glasswings
A Butterfly's Story

Elisa Kleven

Dial Books for Young Readers — an imprint of Penguin Group (USA) Inc.

To Lois Shickman, Kathleen Gulley, and Ashley Bilbao

DIAL BOOKS FOR YOUNG READERS
An imprint of Penguin Young Readers Group
Published by the Penguin Group
Penguin Group (USA) Inc., 375 Hudson Street, New York, New York 10014, USA
Penguin Group (Canada), 90 Eglinton Avenue East, Suite 700, Toronto, Ontario M4P 2Y3, Canada (a division of Pearson Penguin Canada Inc.)
Penguin Books Ltd, 80 Strand, London WC2R 0RL, England
Penguin Ireland, 25 St Stephen's Green, Dublin 2, Ireland (a division of Penguin Books Ltd)
Penguin Group (Australia), 707 Collins Street, Melbourne, Victoria 3008, Australia
(a division of Pearson Australia Group Pty Ltd)
Penguin Books India Pvt Ltd, 11 Community Centre, Panchsheel Park, New Delhi—110 017, India
Penguin Group (NZ), 67 Apollo Drive, Rosedale, Auckland 0632, New Zealand (a division of Pearson New Zealand Ltd)
Penguin Books (South Africa), Rosebank Office Park, 181 Jan Smuts Avenue, Parktown North 2193, South Africa
Penguin China, B7 Jiaming Center, 27 East Third Ring Road North, Chaoyang District, Beijing 100020, China
Penguin Books Ltd, Registered Offices: 80 Strand, London WC2R 0RL, England

Photograph on page 3 © www.shutterstock.com/Wansfordphoto
Designed by Jasmin Rubero
Printed in China

2 4 6 8 10 9 7 5 3 1

Library of Congress Cataloging-in-Publication Data
Kleven, Elisa.
Glasswings : a butterfly's story / by Elisa Kleven.
p.   cm.
Summary: Lost in the city, a butterfly with see-through wings makes friends with a ladybug, an ant,
and a pigeon, and together they help flowers bloom and grow.
ISBN 978-0-8037-3742-6 (hardcover)
[1. Butterflies—Fiction. 2. Flowers—Fiction.] I. Title.
PZ7.K6783875Gl 2013   [E]—dc23   2012017539

The illustrations were made with watercolor, ink , pastel, colored pencils, and scraps of paper and lace.

A note on Glasswings and Pollination

Although Claire is a make-believe butterfly, Glasswings exist in real life! They are hard to spot, though, as they are nearly invisible. Like Claire, they are clear as glass, lacking the colored scales which give other butterflies their brilliant hues and patterns.

Various species of Glasswings can be found in Central and South America, where they are affectionately called *Espejitos*, or "Little Mirrors." Although Glasswings look even more fragile than most butterflies, transparent and delicate as fine glass, their wings are actually quite strong, and they are able to migrate long distances. Glasswings are part of a large family of "brush-footed" butterflies, whose front pair of legs are so tiny that only four legs appear visible.

Like other butterflies, Glasswings are attracted to the bright color and sweet smell of flowers, and they feed on flower nectar. They sip nectar through a mouth part called a proboscis, which resembles a drinking straw and coils up when not in use. As they gather nourishment from flowers, flower pollen sticks to their legs. Butterflies carry this pollen from plant to plant, allowing plants to produce seeds, and new plants to grow. Like bees, butterflies are wonderful pollinators, helping a variety of flowers and plants to thrive.

Perhaps a butterfly near you, transparent or not, is pollinating flowers and keeping the earth healthy and beautiful—great and vital work from such a tiny creature.

Claire was a Glasswing butterfly.
Her wings, as clear as windows,
let the world shine through.

When Claire soared high she looked sky-blue,
or puffy-white, or rainbow-striped.

When she swooped down low
to the forest floor she seemed
as feathery green as the ferns.

And when she fluttered among
the flowers, sipping nectar,
Claire looked like a flower, too.

I like being flowery best, Claire thought.
I love being here with my flowery mother
and father and brothers and sisters
in our bright, blooming home.

But one day, while Claire was chasing a wisp of milkweed silk,

a sudden wind swept her up.

"Claire, we can't see you!" her family called.

"Here I am!" said Claire, but she was lost in the swirling clouds. On and on she tumbled, scared and lonely.

Finally the wind let her go.

She fluttered down to a strange new world,
a city of concrete and corners.

"I hope I'll find some flowers here," Claire said hungrily.

"And I hope that my family will find *me*."

"How would anyone find you?" asked a pigeon.

"You're almost invisible!"

"Your wings are as gray as the sidewalk," a ladybug added.

"As plain as the air," said an ant. "Are you a ghost?"

"Of course not," said Claire. "I'm a Glasswing butterfly.
My wings can be any color at all. Look!"

Claire looked around for a spot of color.

Up above she saw three big ones, lined up in a row.

"Oh!" said the ladybug. "You're as red as *me*, now!"

"And now you're as yellow as a taxi!" cried the pigeon.

"And now you're as green as a soda can!" the ant exclaimed.

"Are you a magic butterfly?"

"I wish," said Claire. "I'd fly right home.

But I don't know the way."

"Stay here with us, then," the pigeon suggested.

"No butterflies ever visit," said the ladybug.

"They just pass overhead, on their way somewhere else."

"Would you like something to eat?" asked the ant,
offering Claire a tortilla crumb.

"Thanks, but I only eat nectar," said Claire. "From flowers."

"Flowers?" asked the pigeon.

"What are flowers?" asked the ant.

"I know what flowers are!" said the ladybug, flapping
her wings. "I ate some tasty aphids on some flowers
just this morning. Follow me, I'll show you."

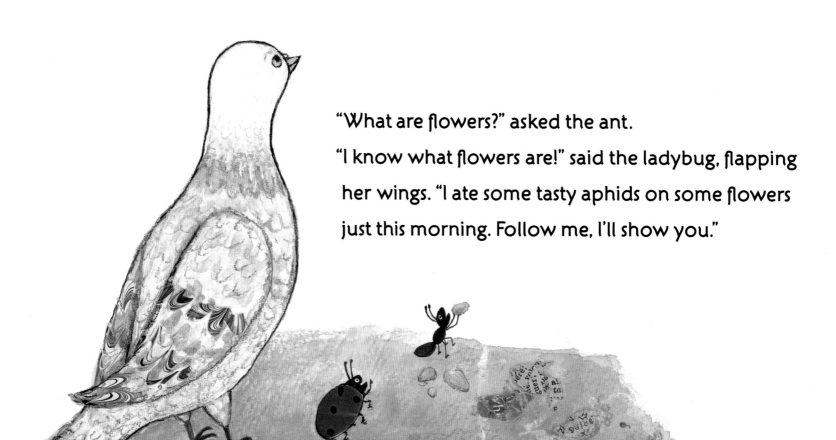

The ladybug led them to an empty lot where
a few flowers grew. They were dusty and
scraggly, nothing like the lush flowers back home.
But they swayed a little in the breeze and offered
Claire their nectar. And as she drank it, Claire felt
more like her old self again.

Day after day, Claire fluttered among the flowers, sipping their nectar, carrying their sticky yellow pollen from plant to plant, helping new flowers to grow.

Her new friends helped the flowers, too. The ladybug kept them free of pests. The ant stirred up the soil they grew in. The pigeon scattered their seeds this way and that.

And Claire was happy with everything
growing and gathering around her.

But at night she dreamed of her family far away.

One morning, the pigeon told Claire,
"Look how many flowers have grown
since you've been here with us!"
"Like magic," said the ant.
"And look at your wings,"
admired the ladybug.

"Look! Look!" said a voice in the sky. Claire looked.

A family of Glasswings was fluttering near.

"Look at that big patch of color!" they cried.

"Look at that flowery butterfly!

She looks just like our . . .

"Here I am!" said Claire. "With my friends."
The butterflies waved their wings. They spun
and swooped through the sky, changing from
blue to gold to purple-pink . . .

starry as the night, sparkly as the city lights,

bright as the butterfly garden

they all make together each day.